FIVE-MINUTE
HALLOWEEN
MYSTERIES

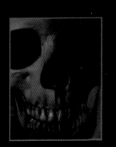

FIVE-MINUTE HALLOWEEN MYSTERIES

BY KEN WEBER

Running Press

Philadelphia • London

Library of Congress Control Number: 2006940118

ISBN 978-0-7624-3076-5

This kit may be ordered by mail from the publisher. Please include
$1.00 for postage and handling.
But try your bookstore first!

Running Press Book Publishers
2300 Chestnut Street
Philadelphia, PA 19103-4371

Visit us on the web!
www.runningpress.com

CONTENTS

THE DRACULA PEOPLE

7

SURPRISE AT ST. CUTHBERT'S

29

THE HALLOWEEN BURIAL

47

SHELTER ON ALL HALLOWS EVE

71

A TIGER IN PARKSIDE ESTATES

85

LOST IN A HALLOWEEN MAZE

107

THE DRACULA PEOPLE

The two police cadets on one side of the old kitchen table were struggling to keep their stomachs under control. Just moments before, on orders from Sir Percy Smythe, they had rolled a body onto its side and saw a human brain for the first time. The fact that the brain was slowly leaking fluid, and that sharp slivers of bone punctuated the mass along with bits of grass and tiny stones, didn't help.

Still, both of them immediately noticed the pair of puncture wounds in the victim's neck, spaced evenly along the jugular vein. The sight made them speak excitedly, one of them in Gaelic, the language in which both felt most comfortable. Sir Percy paid no heed, either to the Gaelic or to the puncture wounds.

"This body was moved," he declared. "Postmortem," he added with an emphatic nod of his over-large head, making it clear that second opinions were unwelcome. Not that either cadet in his wildest dreams would presume to argue with

Scotland Yard's chief criminal investigator. Especially since the famous Sir Percy had journeyed all the way to Kinbraddie, on Scotland's northeast coast, a spot so remote it took several hours by stagecoach to reach from the nearest rail station.

"All right now gentlemen, what is absolutely necessary before we—" Sir Percy had been leaning over the corpse but now stood up abruptly. "Gentlemen! You are utterly without value to a criminal investigation if you don't get close to the crime. Now put your noses here!" He pointed a long bony finger at the victim's head. "Hold those lanterns higher and trim the wicks. We need light! We will never succeed in finding out what happened to this poor fellow and who did it if you continue prancing about like young ponies!"

The "poor fellow" was a local farmer who had been found at first light by a pair of dairymaids on their way to the morning milking. Foul play was certain, but the reason the death was important enough to involve the Yard's top detective was that it was the third murder near Kinbraddie in the past year. Moreover, the killings had attracted attention throughout the whole of the United Kingdom because of a bizarre and very unsettling feature each victim had in common. Like the hapless farmer on the table, each of them had been struck from behind.

That was the cause of death, but in addition to a crushed skull, every one had evenly spaced puncture wounds in the jugular. In a remote, superstitious community like Kinbraddie, it wasn't much of a leap to conclude that a vampire was afoot.

When the lighting improved, Sir Percy's tone softened. "I understand your reluctance, gentlemen. No one enjoys being cozy with a corpse but we must be about our business. Now, where was I? Yes, good. More light. That's better. Now lean closer. Get a good look at that skull. Blunt end of an axe, I'd say, from the shape of the wound. Not that knowing so will help us very much, unless we find an axe with blood and bits of brain. . . . Yes, what is it?"

One of the cadets was visibly agitated. "Speak man!" Sir Percy directed.

"The Dracula People." The cadet spoke so hesitantly in his Scottish brogue that Sir Percy had to lean toward him. "Should we no' be lookin' to them for the axe afore they get too far?" The other cadet nodded vigorously and couldn't resist putting a finger near the puncture wounds. "Aye, the People o' Dracula," he said.

"Ah yes, the gypsies." Sir Percy

sighed long and hard. "You think we should be looking for the gypsies. Even before we know why?"

Encouraged by his response, both cadets began to speak at once. "The blood!" said one.

"Aye, the blood." The other drowned him out. "'Tis well known they be from the land o' Dracula and 'tis them what drinks the blood."

"Do they now?" The older man was skeptical but knew he had to tread carefully as these cadets were local boys. In Kinbraddie, the mysterious ways of the gypsies and their refusal to mix with any but their own kind meant they were blamed for every theft and petty crime for miles around. Even for things like bad weather or cows that wouldn't give milk. The murders added an ominous sheen to the feelings against the gypsies. The second murder led to a near-lynching. This third one could push things over the edge.

"Indeed gentlemen, it is a reasonable strategy you propose." Sir Percy was careful to keep the slightest hint of drama out of his voice. "As you quite rightly informed me, the dairy-maids found our victim beside the gypsy camp, or, I should say, the *former* gypsy camp, since you tell me they left during the night. But the heavy rain last night has made the ground soft and there'll be no trouble following the tracks of the gypsies' big wagons. You are correct, we should search them, just as we should search all the barns and sheds in the neighborhood here. Maybe even the houses."

The cadets started at that but Sir Percy carried on. "But first let us see what our victim has to offer. Every dead body has a story to tell. Now you" he pointed to one of the cadets. "Start with the feet. What do those wellies say?" Very self-consciously, the cadet bent over the Wellington boots. "Wet, like everythin' else," he said, "but not much mud."

"Aha!" Sir Percy made the two jump. "Now what does *that* tell you?"

The same cadet answered. "That . . . 'tis possible he was killed afore the rain come? Else there'd be mud. But he was found on grass. In a cow pasture over beside the Drac . . . er —gypsy camp."

"Indeed." Sir Percy stood in his approval pose, with his arms on his hips. "Lock that away for now. Keep going. What else do you see?"

The second cadet pushed in quickly, not wanting to miss out. "The overalls is wet—from the rain o'course. The shirt's soaked too. Unbuttoned and crumpled. Bits o' grass on the shirttail and . . . and that's blood there with the grass, no?"

"Quite so, very good!" The older man sounded positively triumphant. "More, more! The hands. Always look at the hands." The two cadets competed for the hand nearest them. "Small cut," the victor observed, "on the finger and 'nother on the back. Both healin' though. Nails is broken—and dirty."

"He's a farmer," Sir Percy said, ending any further speculation on the hands. "Now that was good," he continued. "There are no other wounds

I'm sure, but we'll undress him in a minute and go over the entire body again."

He bent over the body to examine the puncture wounds with a large magnifying glass and didn't see the cadets exchange a quick glance at the mention of removing the victim's clothes. "Not a lot of blood left," he noted and moved up to the skull wound. "Nor here, but then there never is." By now the cadets were emboldened by their recent successes so without hesitation one spoke up.

"Well, to be sure there's no blood because the . . . "

"'Twas the Dracula People then what drank his blood, was it not?" the other asked.

Sir Percy made a visible effort to mask his disappointment. "We're not able to put yea or nay to the gypsies yet," he said, "but in my opinion it's not likely. They don't need any more trouble than they have already. The reason there's no blood is this man bled out at the spot where he was killed. It's that place we must find.

And right away. It will show us where to turn next." The cadets spoke as one. "He wasna killed at their camp?"

"The body was moved," Sir Percy spoke sharply. "Postmortem. Weren't you listening?"

What evidence shows that the farmer's body was moved after he was killed?

SOLUTION

The unbuttoned shirt is crumpled with bits of grass and blood on the tail, which shows the body was dragged on its back along the wet grass. The dragging action would bring the shirttail up to the skull wound at the back of the head, accounting for the grass and blood.

Sir Percy is not certain the gypsies are innocent but since they are always suspected of crime, it defies logic to think they would attract attention to themselves by dragging a dead body to their own camp. The puncture wounds on the neck, Percy suspects, are a device to bring the gypsies under suspicion.

Gypsies have lived and wandered across Europe for centuries but as a race and a culture are most frequently associated with Romania. Dracula (historically, Vlad the Impaler) ruled in part of what is modern Romania, in the fifteenth century.

SURPRISE
AT ST. CUTHBERT'S

About a mile from St. Cuthbert's, Rod Sweeney made a sharp right turn into a parking lot and drove to the farthest corner. He wanted to talk to himself in the rearview mirror without anyone seeing what he was doing.

"Look," he said to his reflection as he put the patrol car in Park, "you are thirty-two years old with a family. You have been a cop for seven years, and a good one too. Your colleagues respect you and your family believes in you. This is probably an entirely routine matter and *you* are in charge so take a deep breath and get over to that school!"

The self-scolding seemed to work. Rod straightened in his seat and drove back onto the street, prepared at least for the moment to face his fifth grade teacher, the formidable Sister Agnes. No longer the terror of the fifth grade but now the principal of St. Cuthbert's, Sister Agnes had called the sheriff's department a few moments ago with a request—actually a command—that an officer be dispatched immediately to deal with a matter, in her words, of "grave consequence." Rod got the call.

In the years since he'd graduated from St. Cuthbert's, Rod Sweeney had encountered the tiny nun only twice, but each time she had inspired the same fumbling uneasiness he'd felt every day in the fifth grade. Today, he feared, would be the same, no matter how intensely he lectured himself beforehand.

There was no surprise for him as

he approached the large double doors at the front of his old school. The separate "boys" and "girls" entrances of his day were gone but he knew about that. Nor was there surprise at the level of security; the doors were locked and he had to be buzzed in by someone in the school office. And there was even less surprise when he stepped inside and saw that Sister Agnes, (tipped off by whoever had been on the other end of the intercom) was on her way down the hall to meet him.

"Roderick. We heard you had become a police officer." She paused for a moment, her expression suggesting it was a struggle to come to grips with such an unlikely possibility. Then with one hand she pointed behind her while a ring of keys magically appeared in the other. "This way," she said. Rod followed meekly as she swished back down the hall. Sister Agnes, unlike the other nuns in her order, still wore the traditional flowing black habit.

If not been for the sight he

encountered when she led him into
the storeroom, Rod would have
slipped deep into fifth grade mode
again. The table full of strange
objects, however, pulled him abruptly
into the present, especially the skull,
its hollow eyes and grinning teeth
reminding him that he was a cop and
this was quite possibly an indication
of serious crime.

"Sister Mary Frances. First
grade," sniffed Sister Agnes as if the
name alone explained the bizarre col-
lection. "Since your time." It was

obvious that Rod's former teacher had grave misgivings about Sister Mary Frances.

"Of course, you can see the skull, Roderick. It is why I called the sheriff. The rest of it is all toys and curios, Halloween drivel. I've examined all of it carefully. Except the skull, of course. It is real, is it not? And a human skull?" Rod nodded. The fifth grade memories had totally disappeared.

Sister Agnes's voice suddenly dropped to an uncharacteristic whisper. "It's from Frenchman's Creek, Roderick, the skull. Do you think . . . well it must be part of that . . ." she searched for just the right word, "that *recent discovery*." Her voice recovered its normal timbre once she felt confident with her choice.

The "recent discovery" at Frenchman's Creek was a body. Two fishermen had found it, but rather than notify the sheriff's office, they opted instead to call a local television station which offered a reward for breaking news. The result was that the fishermen got to spend a weekend in Las Vegas while everyone else in Rod's hometown was treated to constant replays of the hapless corpse being raised from the water. What made the news sensational enough to qualify for national coverage as well was that the body was tied to a cement block with loop after loop of fishing line—and the head was missing. Two weeks later the identity of the victim was still a mystery.

Although his first impulse was to return to the patrol car for a pair of rubber gloves, Rod thought better of it when he realized the skull would have who knows how many finger-prints on it by now. Instead, he took out his penknife and tried unsuccess-fully to slide the blade under the fishing line that was tied around the skull. The line crossed over the nose cavity and the cheekbones and was knotted tightly at the back. It was now dried out after having been in water for a time. Several inches of line trailed away from the knot and ended in frayed shreds. Rod could easily see that the skull had once been tied to something but the line had broken.

"I noted the fishing line immediately," Sister Agnes explained, thereby making clear that like everyone else in town, she had followed the news reports very carefully.

Rod gave up on the penknife and put it back in his pocket. He took out his pen and used it to shift around some of the other items on the table so he could get a better look at them. It was a curious array: a conical hat, obviously part of a witch costume, two plastic jack o' lanterns, a shoe with stars painted on it, a bicycle inner tube, the stub of a candle, a very old and faded Roy Rogers holster with no gun in it, a can of—he bent over to be sure—yes, a can of worms, live ones! "Where did all these—?" He wasn't allowed to finish the question.

"Sister Mary Frances." Again, in the mind of Sister Agnes, that was sufficient explanation, but Rod's lifted eyebrows made her carry on.

"Sister teaches the first grade. And yesterday' as you know, was Halloween. The children have been thinking of little else for weeks, no matter how hard we try to distract them." She buried both arms deep into her habit as if the position would shield her from the foolishness of Halloween. "Now what Sister Frances proposed—and I acknowledge that from a certain perspective it has some educational sense to it— she asked the children to bring one item to school today that they could use to tell a story about their Halloween experience." Rod looked at the inner tube and his eyebrows lifted again.

"As I say, it has some sense," Sister Agnes continued. "Usually the children have so much candy and other dreadful sweets that they're all sick to their stomachs by noon, and her idea was to create a distraction. It was the young Ferguson boy, Sean—he is the sixth in the family; there are three more Fergusons here at St. Cuthbert's—he is the one who brought the skull. Sister Frances called me and I called you." She hesitated. "Well, I called the sheriff's office and they sent you. Young Sean is in my office. He says he found it at Frenchman's Creek."

"You did the right thing, Sister." Rod felt good being in control and said it again. "You did the right thing to call us immediately. If you don't mind, I'll use your office to speak to the Ferguson boy now. I'll have to use your telephone too. My cell doesn't work in here and I'll have to get the forensic people involved right away. Incidentally," he went on, "I am confident there is no connection between the skull and the 'recent discovery' at Frenchman's Creek."

"No connection, Roderick? What makes you say that?"

What makes him say that?

SOLUTION

The body discovered by the fishermen two weeks before was weighted down with a cement block and fishing line was used to keep the body and the block together. Since the body was still tied to the block when it was found, it is clear that not a long time had passed between the disposal of the body and its discovery. If a long time had passed between disposal and discovery, the body would have decomposed, or have been eaten by aquatic life in Frenchman's Creek and the fishing line would have been loose as a result. Quite likely, the remains would have become separated from the cement block. In contrast, the line around the skull found by the Ferguson boy was tied tightly to the bone so there was no flesh on the skull when this line was applied. This indicates that the skull comes from a body that met its end quite some time before the body discovered by the fishermen.

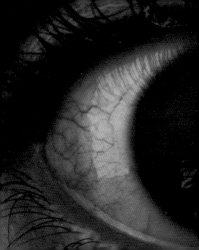

time would not have been able to restore the soil in the precise, natural layers that Marnie saw. Someone—not Marnie's client (he's in jail)—quite likely the killer, put the remains into the trench so that they would be discovered and thereby provide the final step necessary to charge Max Kabovsky with murder.

THE HALLOWEEN
BURIAL

Whitehen her cell phone chirped at 10:30 AM Marnie France didn't bother to look at the call display. She knew this one was coming and as much as she hated to pick up, she knew that leaving it to voice mail would only make things worse.

"Marnie!" It was the gushy voice of Randy Berg. "Sorry to wreck your day babe, but this is big and for sure you want to be the first to know!"

"Randy, I already know . . . "

"Brace yourself, kid. We're

charging your favorite spook this morning, your Goth guy. Murder One!"

"Randy, I . . . "

"Found the body this morning. Well, her skeleton really. Three years in the ground kinda chews away at the skin, doesn't it?"

Marnie took a breath and was about to interrupt, but realized Randy was going to blather away no matter what she said, so she let him carry on. Randy Berg was an assistant district attorney and had a reputation as a force five windstorm. This morning he was right up to speed.

"Before you even think of pleading for a lesser charge, let's get straight on this," Randy was obviously enjoying himself, "there's no question it's your Goth client's dearly departed wife. What did she call herself? The Devil's Spawn? Maybe calling her that was his idea. In any case, he's getting Murder One 'cause it's her for sure; the ring's on the finger, the clothes, the shoes; the other earring's there—inside the skull yet! We'll have dental records by this afternoon. Don't even need DNA. And you know where the Devil's Spawn turned up? Right in their backyard! Not too bright that boy of yours, burying his wife in the backyard."

Randy paused for breath and Marnie jumped in with some force of her own. "Shut up for a minute, Randy! Do you hear me?" She realized she was shouting and made herself count to five under her breath. "To begin with, Assistant

D.A. Berg, I am not a "babe," not yours, not anyone's, and if I hear it one more time, I'll have you up before the ethics committee!" She paused to let complete silence confirm she'd made her point and then continued. "And Mr. Kapovsky is n my 'boy.' He's my client. Furthermore, before you exhaust yourself gloating over the discovery of what *may* be Mrs. Kapovsky's body, I already know all about it. The medical examiner called me ju as she called you."

"Jeez, Marnie," the note of contion in Randy's tone seemed nuine. "I was just trying to give u a heads up before the press got you. For sure they're out there at e farm by now, and you know as ll as I do they're going to make a ss. This Goth person disappears at alloween, and here we are exactly ree years later, Halloween again, d her body turns up. I don't have tell you what that means, do I?"

"Okay Randy, but . . ."

"Let me finish! Please!" Randy's

voice became more business-like. "I also called to tell you we've frozen the site until you come out to see for yourself. Can you meet me there in, say, an hour?"

For a second or two, Marnie thought she might take advantage of the points she'd scored and make Randy wait. Her client, Kapovsky, was in Joyceville, a medium security penitentiary upstate, doing a stretch for fraud and she had a legitimate reason to delay matters so she could first break the news of the discovery to him in person. Thinking rationally though, she knew that getting to see the body—well, skeleton—was important, so she agreed to meet Randy at noon.

Minutes later, as Marnie was settling into her car for the drive out of the city, she realized she hadn't brought the Kapovsky files with her, but just as quickly realized they would not be needed. This was a case she knew like the back of her hand. Three years ago, on Halloween, as Randy Berg had carefully pointed out, Max Kapovsky reported his wife missing. Hours later, her car was found near their country house on a barely passable bush road. That there had been foul play was obvious. There was blood on the driver's seat—hers. The ceiling fabric had been slashed, a single earring lay on the floor and only steps away, the investigating officer found one of her shoes, a low heel pump with a torn strap. But the one element that everyone remembered first, was that in the back seat of the car there was a dead black cat that had apparently been strangled.

The drama of the case was fueled further by the fact that at the time the woman went missing, both Kapovskys had been portraying themselves as Goths and not only maintained a website on the subject but regularly offered their farm as a meeting place. The media naturally focused on high profile features like the Kapovskys' Goth names, the Devil's Spawn and Hollow Man. The police, also naturally, focused on Max as the murder suspect from the beginning, and quite candidly admitted that only the lack of a body kept them from laying a charge. Now, it seemed, the last obstacle to a murder charge had been removed.

Light traffic made it possible for Marnie to reach the Kapovsky farm—*former* Kapovsky farm (it had been sold in the year after the disappearance)—in only forty minutes and she noted with some pleasure that Randy Berg was not yet there. Lots of other activity, however, with police and paramedics everywhere and curious neighbors along the fence. On the south side of the yard, behind the house but east of a large unused barn, Detective-Sergeant Matt Hawkins stood beside a large yellow backhoe. Marnie recognized him right away.

"Ah, Ms. France," the sergeant spoke as Marnie approached. "We've been waiting for you. Please come over here." Matt Hawkins was as polite as Randy was pushy. He gently led Marnie to a narrow trench that began where the excavating bucket of the backhoe rested on the ground and ran all the way to a large barn. Two police officers in plastic coveralls were standing in the trench, their heads just above ground level. Between them was the reason all had gathered there.

"The trench is being dug to put in a water line to the barn," Matt Hawkins explained. He nodded at the backhoe. "Operator turned up the bod—*skeleton* this morning. Kind of weird really. He came in early to get his time in so he could go home and take his kids trick-or-treating tonight and what does he find but this? Actually, he turned up a shoe first, and yeah, it appears to be the match to the one found by her car three years ago. Anyway, then he hit a bone and that's when he called us. We just finished uncovering the remains a few minutes ago. Wasn't that difficult actually because the clothing is still in pretty good shape. You want to take a look now?"

For what seemed like the twentieth time that day, Marnie took a deep breath. She nodded yes and Matt led her gently by the arm to the edge of the trench. Although she had prepared herself for the sight of the skeleton, what impressed her most of all was something she had not anticipated: colors. The bright green grass at the top of the trench on both sides was trampled flat and scored by heel marks and gouges from the backhoe but it was still defiantly and richly green. Beneath the grass was a thin but very precise layer of dark brown

topsoil and under that, almost as if
someone had drawn a horizontal line,
a band of yellow. Sand, Marnie figured. Then, about two feet below
that, right to the bottom of the
trench was the color blue. It was blue
clay, she learned later. The clay softened the ivory hue of the bones and
made the black clothing, dirty as it
was, appear almost, well, elegant.

"See the other earring? Inside
the skull?" The sudden intrusion of
Randy Berg's voice almost made
Marnie pitch into the trench. "Quite

a sight, huh?" Randy was back in force five mode. "Bet your client never expected her to turn up like this, huh? And it almost worked for him too! You see the trench, it was supposed to go over there." Randy waved ambiguously at a spot on the north side of the barn. "But what happened, see, was there's too much rock and tree root over there so the backhoe guy starts trenching right here and *ta da!* Up comes The Devil's Spawn! She's been right in her own backyard all this time waiting for the third anniversary!"

Marnie turned and faced Randy for the first time. Her expression made him turn away. "Mrs. Kabovsky," Marnie spoke through clenched teeth, "and yes, I agree these are probably her remains— Mrs. Kabovsky was not buried here. Not when she died, anyway." She softened both her gaze and her tone as she turned to Sergeant Matt Hawkins. "If you can find out who it was that dumped the skeleton into this trench last night—and we all

know it could not have been my
client, don't we? I'll bet my law
degree it's the same person who
killed Mrs. Kabovsky."

SHELTER ON ALL HALLOWS' EVE

The man concealed behind a tree at the western end of the valley was known in his village as Tabor the Carpenter but at this moment he was far from home and woodwork was the last thing on his mind. He was staring at the remains of a mill several hundred yards down the valley on the south side of the valley floor. For most of the day he had hidden there and for the past hour had not moved a muscle. In fact, the only movement in the valley throughout the entire

day had come from a large flock of
pigeons that had taken up residence
in the mill. From his hiding spot,
Tabor watched the birds strut around
what was left of the roof and once,
when a hawk appeared at the opposite end of the valley, he saw them
rise in a great flutter and dive to
safety in the ruins. Other than that,
the valley was still.

Behind Tabor, about a hundred
yards back, concealed in a small cavity
that months of pounding rain had
etched into the sandy wall of the valley,

a painfully thin woman huddled with her arms around two small children. The woman's name was Esther. She was Tabor's wife, and Adam and Hester were the only two of their four children still alive. Like her husband, Esther was careful to remain utterly quiet lest she be seen. As for the children, starvation had made them too weak to stir.

Tabor and his family were fugitives. Not that they had committed any crime, at least not in their eyes, but they couldn't stay in their village.

Especially on this night, for it was All
Hallows' Eve and Esther was a
witch. Whether she really was a
witch or not (and even Tabor wasn't
entirely sure), what mattered was
that the village believed it. Everyone
knew that on All Hallows' Eve the
spirits of the dead roamed the earth
and if they chose, could wreak
vengeance on anyone who had
wronged them while they were living.
The rains had begun almost two
years ago, bringing on the famine.
Since then, three women had been

burned in the square because of the villagers' firm conviction that they had communed with spirits responsible for the disastrous weather. Two of those women had met their bitter end the previous year on All Hallows' Eve. Tabor knew that this year, Esther's only security lay in flight.

Running made food even harder to come by and for the past week the family had been eating grass, grazing like the scrawny cows that had long disappeared from the land. The diet had nourished Tabor and Esther ever so slightly, but grass made the children so ill that Tabor briefly considered going back to the village, where there was a bit more choice of things to eat. Rats, for example, which were among the reasons for Esther's reputation as a witch. She had convinced the village that roasted rats could be a useful food source. But then after eating one of these over-plentiful vermin, a child had developed fever and a sharp pain in his side that lasted for a day and night and then suddenly disappeared.

An hour later, he was dead.

No, returning to the village was not the answer. There were other problems besides the rats. Although Esther was the one people had always come to for her homemade medicines and salves when they were ill, once the rains started, what had been seen as a gift came to be regarded as a power. And powers, everyone in the village believed, were available only to those who made a deal with the devil. It didn't help her case that Esther was the only woman in the village

who could read, for books could tell of
evil and of spells. And even more con-
demning: for what earthly reason
would a *woman* have been taught to
read if not for nefarious purposes?
Then there was her soft speaking,
communing with no one in particular.
It was the one thing that made Tabor
as uneasy as everyone else in the village. More than once before the rains
he had hidden behind the woodpile
and watched Esther working in their
vegetable garden. It was clear her lips
were moving. She was talking. But to

whom? Esther's simple explanation when he once questioned her—that she talked to herself out of habit—left Tabor unsatisfied.

There was no talking now in the little cave where Esther huddled with Hester and Adam. She didn't have the energy. As for Tabor, he didn't speak much at the best of times. It had been a gray day with thick clouds hanging sullenly in the sky and now that night was approaching, there was a promise of rain, adding more water to a land-scape already clogged with more moisture than it could absorb.

What Tabor, Esther, and the children wanted desperately right now, almost as much as something to eat, was shelter. They had been on the run for days, starving, freezing at night, and constantly in fear of being discovered. Whether they would ever be able to go back to the village was doubtful. Certainly it couldn't happen as long as the weather kept anyone from planting crops. For the moment, what both Tabor and Esther sought was a place to light a fire—some protection from the rain and wind—a shelter entirely to themselves.

For the first time now since they had fled their village in the middle of the night, Tabor felt a tinge of comfort. After watching the ruined mill all day, he knew he had found the very shelter he had been seeking. Not only were there no people at the mill, he was sure that no one had been there for a very long time.

What evidence has led Tabor to this conclusion?

SOLUTION

Pigeons had made a home in the ruined mill. If the famine is so bad that people are eating rats, it is certain anyone living in or near the mill would have caught and eaten these pigeons long before. The mill is empty of people and remote enough to be unknown—a safe spot for now.

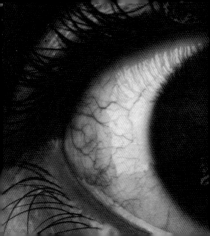

A TIGER IN
PARKSIDE ESTATES

Russell Beresford was wearing a costume—and not because it happened to be Halloween. Not just any costume either; he was dressed as a tiger, complete with a long, swooping tail that thanks to a sturdy interior wire, curved over the back of his neck to his left shoulder, where it was attached with a carefully concealed pin. Normally, Russell would have felt extremely foolish in this getup. It was indeed the first time in his sixty-two years he had worn a costume of any kind. But then, it was also the first time in his life he was going to kill someone, so this was really no time for feelings of embarrassment. In fact, he wasn't even nervous. The pieces were falling into place just as he'd planned.

From where he stood in the copse of spruce trees at the edge of the park, Russell could see across the street. He waited until he saw Barney, the security guard at the entrance to Parkside Estates, leave early for his 7:30 PM break. Right on cue as planned. Now Russell could cross the road, pass unseen through the gate, and be inside his house in one minute and forty-five seconds. He should know. He'd been timing this for months. Another two minutes for Marie; two more to scatter some knick-knacks around——make it look like a break-in; one minute to tape the window and then break it; three minutes to get back here to the park and strip off the dumb tiger costume, and then six more of brisk walking to get across the park and into the card room at the Veterans' Hall. Sixteen minutes, give or take a few seconds. Hard to believe. After forty years of marital agony, it was going to take just sixteen minutes to find peace.

Russell made sure there was no one around before he stepped out of the trees. He looked both ways for traffic before crossing. It was hard to see in the tiger costume as he wasn't just wearing a face mask; the costume covered his head completely. Still, that's what he wanted: to be covered completely. Except for the paws. The ones on his hands he'd discarded and the ones for his feet, which didn't fit over his shoes. The paws didn't matter anyway because of the darkness. He'd even thought of getting rid of the tail because it whipped back and forth as he walked, but a tailless tiger might be easier to remember.

Once he was sure the road was clear, Russell crossed quickly. So far so good. Barney might have been a problem if he had not left early for his break, as he usually did. Even with the tiger costume. When Russell had left Parkside Estates just before 7 PM for his regular evening stroll he'd stopped for a chat with Barney, thereby creating a witness, should one be necessary, to testify that Russell Beresford had left Parkside Estates. But if Barney had stayed at his post until 7:30 as he was supposed to, Russell would have had to walk past him in the tiger outfit to stay on schedule. Not a good idea, but getting back into the gated community, dealing with Marie, and then getting back out and over to the Veterans' Hall ahead of the others was all a matter of timing, and he had been prepared to take the chance.

The bit at the coffee shop on the other side of the park had gone smoothly too. Russell had never actually been in the shop, but over the past six months he had made a point of waving to the ladies working inside. Sometimes he would stop at the big plate-glass window and sometimes he'd wave from across the street. For some reason, just like tonight, the coffee shop was never busy at this time and the ladies usually noticed and waved back. Sometimes, he knew, they didn't see him or perhaps they just ignored him—but Russell felt that was all right too. All that mattered was that in their minds there was this old guy out for a walk who waved to them every evening.

Once inside the gate, Russell needed only a bit of time to get to his house. Parkside Boulevard was the main thoroughfare that ran east from the entrance and wound serpent-like through the Estates. The Beresfords,

Russell and Marie, had bought 5 Weyburn Place several years ago. Their street was the first one inside the gates leading south from the Boulevard. From the location it was easy to get over to the large city park next door. Between each property in Parkside Estates, a cedar hedge promoted a sense of privacy for the residents, except at Numbers 3, 5, and 7 Weyburn Place. That was because of Mrs. Krefchik in Number 4. She made a career of keeping an eye on the three houses across the street. Mrs. Krefchik missed nothing and was the most important reason for the tiger costume.

Russell had learned from months of observation that Barney could be relied upon to shirk his duties if only because his supervisor was even more lax. Leaving early at break time was a case in point. Barney was supposed to stay at the gate until precisely 7:30 and the supervisor was supposed to relieve him for fifteen minutes. But ever since last August, when Ineda Mann had begun working the six to eleven shift at the lunch counter in the Parkside Rec Center, the guarding of the gate had suffered a serious decline. Instead of relieving Barney, the supervisor had been spending the entire time on a counter stool basking in the charms of Ms. Mann, and even the increasingly early arrival of Barney to share the glow of her company, hadn't had the least impact on his neglect of duty.

No, the security staff was no problem. Mrs. Krefchik, however, did represent a threat. If anyone was going to see Russell this night and note the details of his coming or going, it would be his impossibly nosy neighbor. Krefchik, therefore, was the principal reason that Marie would meet her fate on Halloween night. In the dark, Russell had reasoned, and amid the general confusion caused by a lot of other people roaming the streets in costumes, a short person in a tiger suit would simply be part of the landscape, safe from the prying eyes at Number 4 Weyburn Place.

The strategy seemed to work.

When Russell emerged from the north side of the hedge at Number 3 he looked like any other trick-or-treater. Walking nonchalantly, he went right past his own house—Number 5 was completely dark, a message to Halloween creatures that they would be wasting their time knocking on this door—and turned into Number 7. He quickly hurried along the hedge to the rear, crossed his own yard to the back door of his house, and slipped inside.

Marie lay stone still on the couch

as if she had read a script and was cooperating fully, but then that was one part of his plan Russell knew he could count on completely. Marie had begun passing out earlier in the day over the past year. Russell thought it may have been the switch to gin. Seems she couldn't handle it like the bourbon. In any case, she was sprawled out now in exactly the same position as when he'd left and with almost magical coordination, there was still a drink in her hand.

The next three steps went

entirely without a hitch. Marie didn't
even struggle when Russell pressed
the cushion down on her face and
held it there. Trashing the room as
kids or maybe a spaced out druggie
might do it was quick, but Russell
had rehearsed that part in his mind so
he knew well ahead of time what to
do. The final move took only seconds.
He slipped out to the porch, peeling
several strips from a roll of masking
tape. Then, after putting the strips
on the back window to control broken glass, he smashed a hole in the

window just large enough for a person's arm to reach inside and undo the window latch. Russell paused for a few seconds to admire the results. Just as he'd planned, it looked like a typical break and enter job.

Exiting Parkside Estates was as uneventful as getting in. The guard's post was still empty (Russell said a silent thank you to Ms. Mann) and although there was more traffic on the street now, there were dozens of costumed trick-or-treaters as well, so he was confident no one was paying particular attention to a tiger.

In the copse of spruce trees at the edge of the park, Russell gratefully stripped off his costume, put it in a plastic grocery bag, and with it tucked under his arm, headed off in the darkness toward the Veterans' Hall. This was one part he had worried about because the only lighting in the park was on the walkways. There was no way he was going to let himself be seen on his walk to the Hall, which meant he would have to find his way through the wooded area.

As it turned out, he stumbled once over a tree root but didn't fall and before long, the lights of the Hall were in view.

Before slipping in a back door to avoid the reception area, Russell tossed the tiger costume into a dumpster at the edge of the parking lot. Then on his way to the card room, he quietly opened the door to the utility closet and put the roll of masking tape back where he'd picked it up last night. When he entered the card room and saw that he was the first one there, he knew his plan had worked. Barney had seen him leave; the coffee shop ladies would verify he was out in the park; no one had seen him in the Estates, and his buddies would testify that he was in the Vet Hall. It was foolproof. Only after he'd finished dealing himself a hand of solitaire did he feel sheer panic. It was then that he realized he'd made a major mistake.

What was Russell Beresford's mistake?

SOLUTION

When Russell put tape on the window, he left his fingerprints all over it. There was no reason to wear gloves for the murder because it was natural for his prints to be all over the house, including the window. But not on the tape.

LOST IN A
HALLOWEEN MAZE

"I'm scared, Tabby." DeDe Cass spoke in a whisper, as if by being quiet she wouldn't upset whatever spooky forces were lurking nearby in the tall stalks of corn. "I'm scared," she repeated. "This isn't fun anymore. And it's getting really dark. I want out of here!"

Tabitha Curzoni didn't answer. In the dim light, she was studying a small sign painted on a piece of cardboard and nailed to a wooden stake. The sign was something Tabitha had never seen before, but she was sure it was a code.

Tabitha and
DeDe had sneaked
into the cornfield
maze some time ago
and immediately
became lost. Over the
past hour they had
encountered other signs too. None of
them were the same, but all of them,
like this one, were stuck into the
ground precisely at a point where the
path they followed split in two. Once
again there was a decision to be

made: take the route to the right or the one to the left. Tabitha knew she would have to be the one to make that decision.

"*Tabby!*" DeDe was considerably louder this time. "Come on! Let's get out of here!"

There was still no answer from Tabitha. Not that she was unafraid, but experience had taught her that in tight spots, she would be the one to make decisions. Leadership was not part of DeDe's makeup. The two were best friends. Their teachers at

Franklin Pierce Grammar School
described them as "joined at the
hip," although one of the more cyni-
cal staff members had once noted
that "joined at the brain" would be a
better description, given that DeDe
appeared incapable of functioning on
her own and followed her best friend
like a puppy.

The girls had encountered the
first of these signs only a few minutes
after entering the cornfield maze.
Like the ones that followed, the first
was painted on stiff cardboard and

nailed to a stick. It was an odd symbol with two arrows, pushed into the ground at a point in the maze where the path forked. The sign offered two choices: go right or go left.

Without explaining her strategy, Tabitha had immediately led her best friend down the path to the left, but after numerous sharp-angled turns and false archways, it came to a dead end so that there was no alternative but

to retrace their steps—if that was possible! True to form however, as they had proceeded along the tunnel, the ever-thoughtful Tabitha had dropped tiny shreds of paper torn from a note in the pocket of her jeans. Using these bits to guide them, the girls had no trouble finding their way back to the sign and this time took the tunnel to the right.

When they reached another sign and once again had to choose between paths to the right and left, both girls knew their situation now carried a hint of uncertainty. Like the first sign, this one, again on cardboard and nailed to an upright stick in the ground, appeared to be some kind of code.

When DeDe asked whether Tabitha had more notepaper to spread along the path to the left again, the answer she got was curt enough to force her into silence. DeDe wasn't used to being spoken to so sharply by her best friend but then being DeDe, she hadn't yet figured out three important things: one, that the solid and reliable Tabitha was getting anxious—it had, after all, been her idea to sneak into the maze after it was closed—and two, that if they didn't get out of the maze soon, they would be in total darkness. There was no artificial light and no houses nearby as the maze was in a huge field far from town. The third thing DeDe had not yet thought about was that if they didn't make it out of the maze, there was not going to be any dramatic rescue until morning.

For a second time, the left path proved to be a dead end, and once again Tabitha's notepaper led them back to the starting point. This time she picked up the paper as they returned, adding to the time that it took to get down the right path, and eventually, to the next sign. The paths, it seemed, were now more complex, with many more false openings and turnings. By now, even DeDe knew they were in trouble.

"Tabby," she said, at first silently, almost to herself, until she realized that her suspicion could very well be real. "*Tabby!*" Much louder this time. "What if there's snakes?"

"There are no snakes," Tabitha answered, staring for a moment at the corn that surrounded them. The stalks were tall, at least twice her height and planted thickly. There was clearly no hope of getting out of the maze by any means other than the correct path.

"What do you mean there are no

snakes? This is Tennessee! We have snakes in this state! And we're in a cornfield!"

"Don't make so much noise! We . . . Look!"

Unlike the previous signs, the stick holding this one was tilted to the left. Otherwise, it was similar to the others: a strange symbol with a pair of arrows pointing in opposite direc-

tions. And once again, there was a choice of two paths: right and left.

"They come out at night, don't they? Snakes, I mean." DeDe wasn't finished. "Tabby, I don't care if we do the maze before our class does it tomorrow, I just want to get out before we run into any snakes."

The girls' scheme—or rather Tabitha's—which had seemed like a great idea when they first biked out to the cornfield, was to get into the maze and have it figured out before they came on a field trip the next day with their class. The maze had been designed and planted by a local service club for Halloween fun and was already a hit in communities for miles around, even though the big night was still a week away.

DeDe's complaints seemed to have little effect on Tabitha as she knelt to examine the sign, thinking maybe the tilt was a clue. "It's been bumped, or knocked over," she concluded, moving the stick back and forth like a loose tooth. "To the left again, she said, "hurry!" This time she was careful to place the bits of paper so they could be more easily seen in the dimming light and this time again, she had to gather them up as once more, the route to the left proved to be the wrong one.

It was when the two girls came to the next sign, that DeDe dug in her heels. When Tabitha said they would start with the path to the right this time because it was almost completely dark now and all the others had gone that way, DeDe spoke.

"No. This time we go to the left,"

she announced in a tone so firm that Tabitha wondered if she was imagining it. "The left," DeDe repeated.

"What makes you think . . . "

"It's a code, Tabby, can't you see? We follow the code and it tells us which path to take so we can get out of the maze. I can even tell you what the next sign will be—if there is another sign before the exit. And if there's a sign after that I can tell you what that one will look like too! Now follow me!"

Why does DeDe want to take the path to the left? And what will the next sign be if there is one?

SOLUTION

The signs are mirrored numbers in sequence. The very first sign is the number 1. Its true image is on the right (the correct path to take) and its mirrored image is on the left (the dead end path). The second sign is the mirrored number 2, again with the true image on the right and the mirrored, or false image, on the left. The same is true for the sign bearing the

number 3. In each case the path
to the left, the mirrored side,
turned out to be wrong. But at
the fourth sign, the number 4, the
true image this time is on the left.
DeDe wants to go that way. (If
there is another
sign before they
reach the exit it
will be the number
five and they will
have to go to the
right.)

This book has been bound using handcraft methods and Smyth-sewn to ensure durability

Cover designed by Bill Jones

Interior Design by Debbie Carleton.

Illustrations by Bill Jones

Edited by Cindy De La Hoz

The text was set in Bodoni, and Spartan Four MT.